LITTLE HOUSE
Laura Ingalls Wilder

MY FIRST LITTLE HOUSE BOOKS

SUMMERTIME ∾ IN THE ∾ BIG WOODS

ADAPTED FROM THE LITTLE HOUSE BOOKS

By Laura Ingalls Wilder

Illustrated by Renée Graef

HARPERCOLLINS PUBLISHERS

For Maggie
—R.G.

Special thanks to Marty Perkins of Old World, Wisconsin.

Summertime in the Big Woods Text adapted from Little House in the Big Woods, copyright 1932, 1960 Little House Heritage Trust Illustrations copyright © 1996 by Renée Graef Manufactured in China . All rights reserved. Library of Congress Cataloging-in-Publication Data. Wilder, Laura Ingalls, 1867–1957. Summertime in the Big Woods / adapted from the Little house books by Laura Ingalls Wilder ; illustrated by Renée Graef. p.   cm. — (My First Little House books) Summary : A little girl and her pioneer family spend a summer in the Big Woods of Wisconsin. ISBN 0-06-025934-5 ISBN 0-06-443497-4 (pbk.) [1. Summer—Fiction. 2. Frontier and pioneer life—Wisconsin—Fiction. 3. Family life—Wisconsin— Fiction. 4. Wisconsin—Fiction.] I. Graef, Renée, ill. II. Title. III. Series. PZ7.W6461Su 1996 E—dc20 94-48814 CIP   AC   Typography by Christine Kettner   17 SCP 10 9 8   ❖   First Edition For information address HarperCollins Children's Books, a division of HarperCollins Publishers, 195 Broadway, New York, NY 10007.

HarperCollins®, ✸, and Little House® are trademarks of HarperCollins Publishers Inc. www.littlehousebooks.com

Illustrations for the My First Little House Books are inspired by the work of Garth Williams with his permission, which we gratefully acknowledge.

Once upon a time, a little girl named Laura lived in the Big Woods of Wisconsin in a little house made of logs. She lived in the little house with her Pa, her Ma, her big sister Mary, her little sister Carrie, and their good old bulldog Jack.

It was summertime in the Big Woods, and the whole family was very busy. Pa worked hard all day long in the fields.

Laura and Mary helped Ma weed the garden.
They helped her feed the calves and the hens.
They helped her gather the eggs.

Summer was also the time for visitors. When company came to visit, Ma would do some extra cooking and cleaning, and there would be new children for Laura and Mary to play with.

Sometimes Ma let Laura and Mary go visiting by themselves. They would walk across the road and up the hill to visit Mrs. Peterson.

Mrs. Peterson's house was always very neat, because she had no little girls to muss it up. She always gave Laura and Mary a cookie when they left, and they nibbled the cookies very slowly while they walked home.

Laura nibbled away exactly half of her cookie, and Mary nibbled away exactly half of her cookie. They saved the other halves to give to Baby Carrie when they got home.

When the summer grass was tall and thick
in the woods, and the cows were giving plenty of
milk, that was the time for Ma to make cheese.

Laura and Mary were always there when Ma made the cheese, helping all they could. They loved to eat bits of the cheese curd. It squeaked in their teeth.

One day Pa came home at noon with a surprise. He had found a bee tree! The wagon was filled with buckets and pails, all heaping full of dripping, golden honeycomb.

For dinner they all had as much of the delicious honey as they could eat, and Pa told them about the bee tree.

He told them that the whole tree was hollow, and filled from top to bottom with honey. Laura felt sorry for the bees. But Pa told her there was lots of honey left for them.

After dinner Ma washed the dishes, and Laura and Mary helped. The dishes made little cheerful sounds as Laura and Mary wiped them. The windows were wide open to the warm summer night.

Soon Laura and Mary were tucked in their beds listening to Pa whistling softly to himself. It had been another happy summer day in the little house in the Big Woods.